STARTING
SCHOOL

Story by MURIEL STANEK

Pictures by BETTY & TONY DELUNA

ALBERT WHITMAN & COMPANY, CHICAGO

To Becky Rosdahl, with love

Text © 1981 by Muriel Stanek
Illustrations © 1981 by Betty and Tony DeLuna
Published simultaneously in Canada by
General Publishing, Limited, Toronto
All rights reserved. Printed in U.S.A.

10 9 8 7 6 5 4 3

Library of Congress Cataloging in Publication Data
Stanek, Muriel.
  Starting school.

  (Self-starter books)
  SUMMARY: The young narrator describes classroom
activities during the first day of school.
  [1. School stories] I. DeLuna, Betty. II. Deluna,
Tony. III. Title.
PZ7.S78637St   [E]   81-297
ISBN 0-8075-7617-4   AACR1

"In the fall you'll start school," Mama
says one day. "It's time to get ready."

She shows me the way to walk there.

We go inside and look around.

"This will be your room," Mama says.
We peek in and see the children working.

The teacher comes to the door to meet us.

"I can hardly wait for school to start,"
I tell her.

All summer I get ready.

Daddy listens while I count to ten and
say my address and telephone number.

I show him how I write my name.

Mama takes me to the doctor for a
school checkup.

And I visit the dentist.

Daddy and I go shopping for new school
shoes. I get to choose the color I like.

I show Daddy how I can tie my shoes all
by myself. I can zip my jacket, too.

"I'm ready," I tell Mama and Daddy on
the first day of school.

"You bet you are!" Daddy laughs.

Mama says, "This is your big day. Come,
I'll walk with you to school."

At the door to my room, Mama says,
"Goodbye, honey! Be good!"

I don't cry, but Mama does.

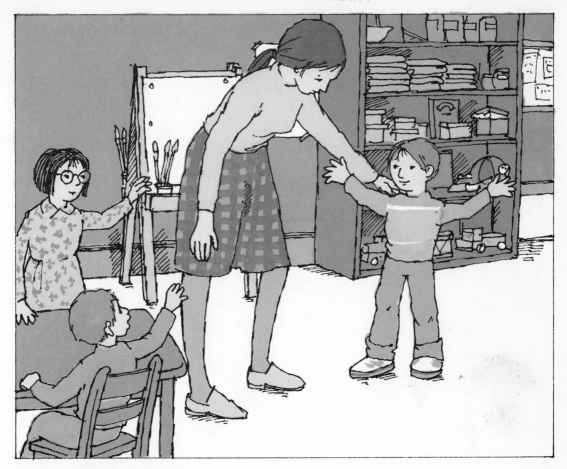

I go inside. The teacher says, "I'm glad to see you."

My friends Timmy and Mary are already there.
I say "hi" and sit down beside them.

One boy tries to run out. He wants to go
home with his mother. But the teacher takes
him by the hand and brings him back in.

When all the children are in their seats,
she says, "Good morning, boys and girls.
I'm Mrs. Baker. Let's see who's here today."

She calls our names, and everyone answers
"here."

Suddenly we hear a funny scratching noise,
and in runs Timmy's dog. "Bowwow! Bowwow!"
he barks as he runs around the room.

"Go home, Pal," says Timmy. "Go home!"
He takes Pal outside.

Then I look around at all the things in the room.

"What's this?" I ask the teacher.

"A hamster," she answers. "Would you
like to help take care of him?"

"Okay," I tell her.

"What does the sign say?" I ask again.
"It says SCIENCE TABLE," she tells me.

I pick up a glass and look at things
under it. Everything looks big.

The teacher gives us paper and crayons
for drawing.

At home, I have all the crayons for myself.
At school, we share them. But Danny wants
to keep the red. I tell him I want a turn, too.

When it's story time, everyone sits on the
floor near the teacher's chair. I sit very
close to her, and she smiles at me. She
reads a story called *Millions of Cats*.

"Read it again," Mary asks.
"Tomorrow," the teacher says. "Now
it's time to sing."

We sing and clap to "Pop Goes the Weasel."
Danny stomps his feet so hard, the teacher
says, "Sh! Sh!"

After a while the teacher lines us up,
and we walk to the water fountain.
Danny says he's first, but he isn't.
I push him a little. The teacher puts
us both at the end of the line.

When it's time to work, Danny and I help
each other. We mark the pictures that
look alike, and I write my name at
the top of my paper.

Then a loud bell rings, and the teacher
says, "Time to go home." We walk down
the hall with our partners.

Mama's waiting at the door. "Here are the
papers I made," I call out to her.
"Did you do this all by yourself?" she asks.
"Sure," I answer. "Won't Daddy be surprised?"

As we walk home, she asks,
"How's your teacher?"
"Fine," I say. "I think she likes me."
"How can you tell?" asks Mama.
"Because she calls me 'Honey,' just
the way you do," I say.

The next morning I ask Mama, "Can I
go to school alone today?"
"Well," she says, "will you promise
to be careful?"
"Yes, yes," I promise her.

Mama stands in front of our house and watches as I walk down the street. When I come to the corner, I look back and wave.

Then I go the rest of the way by myself.

DATE DUE

APR 28 '88			
SEP 14			